This book belongs to

....

Walt Disney's

Mary Poppins
Takes a Jolly Holiday

Storybook Favourites

Reader's Digest Young Families

Walt Disney's
Mary Poppins
Takes a Jolly Holiday

Illustrations by The Walt Disney Studios

Illustrated by Beverly Edwards and Leon Jason

Based on the Walt Disney Motion Picture

Story adapted by Annie North Bedford

$\mathcal{M}$ary Poppins, the new nanny, had just taught Jane and Michael Banks a game called 'Well Begun Is Half Done,' or 'Tidy Up The Nursery.' It was such fun that when it was over and the nursery was as neat as a new pin, Michael wanted to do it all over again.

'Nonsense!' said Mary Poppins. 'Spit-spot! Time for an outing in the park!' And Michael and Jane in their hats and coats followed at her heels out through the gate and into Cherry Tree Lane.

Once outside in the lane, Mary walked off so quickly that Jane and Michael had to skip to keep up. But at the entrance to the park, she stopped. For there was Bert, a jack of all trades – someone who could do just about anything! Bert was kneeling down on the pavement, drawing pictures in coloured chalk.

The pictures were lovely. There was one of boats on the river, and another of a circus – not a very large circus, but still, there was a lion and a tiger, and a man on a unicycle. Michael stopped to admire it. But Jane strolled on. All at once she stopped too. 'Oh, this is a lovely one,' she said. 'I'd like to go there.'

'A typical English countryside,' said Bert proudly. 'What's more, though you can't see it, there's a little country fair down that road and over the hill. Quite a splendid place for travel and high adventure, I should say.'

'May we go, Mary Poppins? Please,' begged Michael.

'I have no intention,' said Mary Poppins, 'of making a fool of myself, thank you.'

'Then,' said Bert with a wink for Michael and Jane, 'I'll do it myself.'

'Do what?' asked Michael.

'A bit of magic,' said Bert, taking each child by a hand. 'It's easy! You wink … You think … You do a double blink … You close your eyes and – jump!'

'Really!' sniffed Mary Poppins. But she put up her umbrella. And away they all went, straight into the typical English countryside.

It was a lovely spot, green and quiet and sparkling with sun. And Bert and Mary Poppins were wearing beautiful clothes. Bert had an entirely new outfit and, best of all, a new straw hat. Mary Poppins was dressed in the height of fashion, from her wide-brimmed bonnet to the diamond buttons shining on her shoes. Jane and Michael looked just as elegant.

'I thought you said there was a fair,' said Michael, who was not impressed by fine clothes.

'So I did,' Bert answered with a smile. 'Down the road and over the hill. Don't you hear the music of the merry-go-round?'

And all at once they did. So over the hill ran Michael and Jane.

'My,' said Mary Poppins, as Bert took her arm and they set off down the little country road, 'I might be having my day out. This is quite a holiday.'

At the word, Bert clicked his dancing heels and tuned up his voice in song. 'Any day with Mary,' sang Bert, 'is a jolly holiday.'

'Now this *is* lovely!' said Mary Poppins, which showed that she was really pleased.

And all the animals of the countryside came out to greet Mary Poppins. The lambs with hearts so light, the cow all brown and white, the horse so good and grey, and the geese all came to say, 'Any day with Mary is a jolly holiday.'

'Nothing makes a holiday complete,' said Bert, 'like a spot of afternoon tea.' He waved his arm and there before them, in an open place filled with sunlight, stood a tea pavilion.

'Strike me pink!' said Mary Poppins. That was what she said when she was especially pleased.

Soon they were seated at the best table, with waiters hopping about to serve them.

'Now then,' said Mary Poppins, studying the menu. 'What would be nice? Some raspberry ice cream and fairy cakes, and tea?'

'Anything for you, Mary Poppins,' said the waiter, who looked exactly like a penguin. 'Order what you will. There will be no bill. It's com-pli-men-ta-ry.'

When their tea was finished, Bert and Mary waltzed away; it was much too jolly a holiday to walk in the usual way. Down the road they went to the merry-go-round.

The merry-go-round slowed down as they approached it. They leaped aboard, landing gracefully on the horses' backs. Jane and Michael were ever so pleased to see them.

'Imagine!' said Jane. 'Our own private merry-go-round. Oh, this is such fun!'

'Very nice,' said Bert, in a posh sort of way. 'Very nice indeed – that is, if you don't want to go anywhere.'

'Who says we're not going anywhere?' said Mary Poppins with a toss of her head. And she had a word with the guard.

'Right-o, Mary Poppins,' he smiled and lifted his cap. Then he pulled the tallest lever on the merry-go-round machine – and off went their horses, *tum-tum-tee-tum,* across the countryside.

In the distance a hunting horn sounded. 'Follow me!'
Mary Poppins called over her shoulder. And away they rode
to the call of the horn, passing huntsmen and hounds and all.
As they galloped on past, Bert even reached down and scooped
up the fox for a ride.

They were travelling so fast that the children scarcely noticed
that Mary Poppins had left their side.

Suddenly Mary Poppins was in the middle of a horse race, and being Mary Poppins, she won.

While Mary Poppins received congratulations on her splendid victory, Jane and Michael watched from the top of a fence where they sat eating toffee apples with Bert. It was then that the first raindrops fell.

There was a flash of lightning, then a sudden downpour.
They all huddled close under Mary Poppins' umbrella, while
all around the countryside seemed to run together. Mary Poppins'
pretty bonnet melted, and the diamonds vanished from the
buttons on her shoes.

Jane and Michael looked away politely … Why, there was the
park! They were standing by the road just around the corner
from Cherry Tree Lane. And on the pavement Bert's drawings
were vanishing into bright puddles of rain.

'Oh, Bert,' said Mary Poppins, 'all your fine drawings ...'

'There are more where they came from, Mary, my dear,' said Bert. And he smiled at her as if in his eyes she still wore the lovely bonnet and fine clothes and the diamond buttons on her shoes.

'Hurry along, children,' said Mary Poppins. 'Spit-spot or we shall be late for tea. Good-bye, Bert.'

And she smiled at him. She was still smiling, was Mary Poppins, when they turned into Cherry Tree Lane.

Soon they were snug in the nursery once more, with a fire glowing in the fireplace. On the hearth stood their three pairs of shoes, drying out from the dash through the rain. Beside them leaned Mary Poppins' umbrella. The parrot on its handle was blinking sleepily.

Tea was over and Mary Poppins was tucking Michael and Jane into bed.

'I shall never be able to sleep,' said Jane. 'So many lovely things have happened today.'

'I beg your pardon?' said Mary Poppins.

'Why, when we rode the merry-go-round,' said Jane with a yawn. 'And the horses jumped off and raced across the countryside,' Michael broke in. 'And you won the big race, Mary Poppins!'

'A respectable person like me,' gasped Mary Poppins, 'in a horse race? What a suggestion!'

'But it did happen!' Michael insisted, sitting straight up in bed. 'I saw it! And I don't want to go to sleep.'

'Very well,' said Mary Poppins. 'Suit yourselves.' She sat in her rocking chair and began to sing softly:

'Stay awake, don't rest your head,
Don't lie down upon your bed.
While the moon drifts in the skies,
Stay awake, don't close your eyes.'

But Jane and Michael did not hear her. For they were fast asleep.

Walt Disney's Mary Poppins Takes a Jolly Holiday is a *Disney Storybook Favourites* book

Taken from *Walt Disney's Mary Poppins A Jolly Holiday,* copyright © 1964, 2006 Disney Enterprises, Inc.
Based on the Walt Disney Motion Picture and the original Mary Poppins stories by P.L.Travers.
Story adapted by Annie North Bedford.
Illustrations by Beverly Edwards and Leon Jason.

This edition was adapted and published in 2009 by
The Reader's Digest Association Limited
11 Westferry Circus, Canary Wharf, London E14 4HE

Editor: Rachel Warren Chadd
Designer: Louise Turpin
Design consultant: Simon Webb

® Reader's Digest, the Pegasus logo and Reader's Digest Young Families
are registered trademarks of
The Reader's Digest Association, Inc.

We are committed both to the quality of our products
and the service we provide to our customers.
We value your comments, so please do contact us on
08705 113366 or via our website at
www.readersdigest.co.uk
If you have any comments or suggestions
about the content of our books, email us at
gbeditorial@readersdigest.co.uk

Printed in China

A Disney Enterprises/Reader's Digest Young Families Book

ISBN 978 0 276 44478 4
Book code 641-037 UP0000-1
Oracle code 504400088H.00.24